Jon Scieszka
Illustrated by David Shannon

SIMON & SCHUSTER BOOKS FOR YOUNG READERS → An imprint of Simon & Schuster Children's Publishing Division → 1230 Avenue of the Americas, New York, New York 10020 → Text copyright © 2009 by Jon Scieszka → Illustrations copyright © 2009 by David Shannon → All rights reserved, including the right of reproduction in whole or in part in any form. → SIMON & SCHUSTER BOOKS FOR YOUNG READERS is a trademark of Simon & Schuster, Inc. → Book design by Dan Potash → The text for this book is set in PlatformOne. → The illustrations for this book are rendered in acrylic on illustration board. → Manufactured in the United States of America

2 4 6 8 10 9 7 5 3 1

Library of Congress Cataloging-in-Publication Data → Scieszka, Jon. → Robot Zot! / Jon Scieszka ; illustrated by David Shannon. → p. cm. → Summary: Arriving in a suburban kitchen, their first stop on a mission to conquer planet Earth, tiny but brave Robot Zot and his mechanical sidekick, Bot, battle fearsome kitchen appliances. → ISBN: 978-1-4169-6394-3 [hardcover : alk. paper] → [1. Robots—Fiction. 2. Humorous stories.] I. Shannon, David, 1959– ill. II. Title. → PZ7.S41267Ro 2009 → [E]—dc22 → 2008020031

For Pops
—D. S.

For Don Q.
and Sancho P.
—J. S.

Simon & Schuster Books for Young Readers · New York · London · Toronto · Sydney

"Robot Zot— Wham Bot! Robot Zot— Bam Bot!"

"No one stop Robot Zot.
Robot Zot crush lot!"

Robot Zot strikes. He crashes his Attack Ship into the heart of the dangerous Earth Army.

Zot howls his brave battle cry:

"Robot Zot—never fall. Robot Zot—conquer all!"

Zot leaps to the attack.

Zot defeats them.
Every one.

"Affirmative."

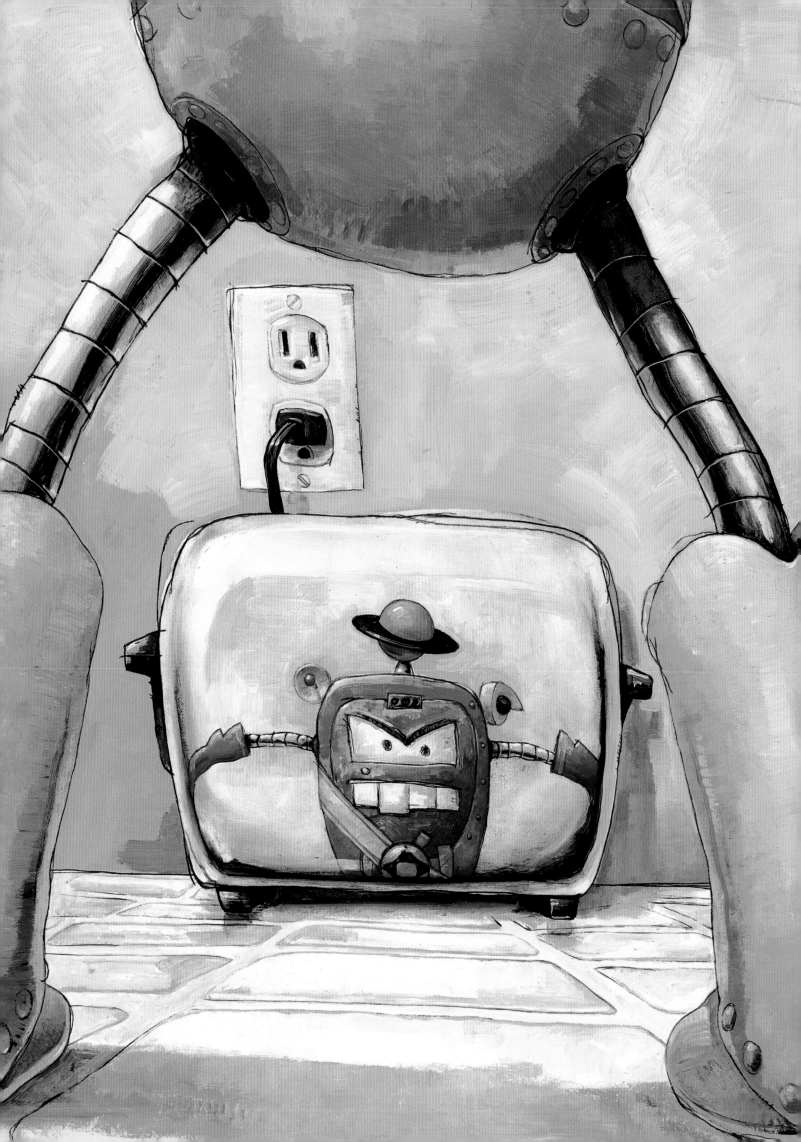

Zot challenges Earth's shiny Captain.
"You are looking at Zot, tough guy?"
Zot blasts the Captain.
The Captain blasts back, then blows a fuse.

"Robot Zot—Hot Bot!"

Zot scans the battlefield. He is glorious.
He stands victorious.

But then, from the upper level of the Earth Fortress, a foul challenge rings forth.

"IS YOUR BREATH NOT SMELLING AS FRESH AS YOU WOULD LIKE?"

"You say what?" beeps Zot. "Prepare to battle!"

"MAYBE YOU SHOULD TRY LEMONMINTPINEFRESH!"

"Maybe you should shut transmission sender," growls warlord Zot.

Zot fights his way through the coils of another Earth monster to get at the insulting enemy.

Zot challenges his gigantic foe.

"Aha," says Robot Zot. "Who is talking large now?"

"ONE QUICK SPRITZ IN THE MORNING . . . "

"Stop transmission. Or Robot Zot will *wham* your bot."

"Zot was not joking.
Zot is never joking."

Zot blasts into another bunker. And there he sees her. The most amazing Earth person . . . ever.

Zot knows that she is the Queen of all Earth.

Brrring, brrring! rings the Queen.

"What?" asks Zot. "Earth Queen held captive? Needs Zot's help to escape?"

For the first time ever, Zot feels something more than war in his machinery.

"Mama," growls the evil guard on her left.
"Dada," warns the scary sentry on her right.
Zot freezes. Even Zot is scared.
Zot says what he has never said.
"Wow. Even Zot is scared."
"Maybe leave? Just go home now? Mission over?"
Brrring, brrring! rings the Queen.
The terrible guards fall on her.

"Wait. What is Zot? Chicken Bot?"

"No!" he booms.
"Zot must be

Hero Bot!"

Robot Zot does not fall.
Robot Zot conquers all!

Lionhearted Robot Zot rescues
his Queen.
They blast and shoot and
wham and bam and battle their
way back to Zot's ship.
Zot sings his victory song:

"No one can stop
Robot Zot!"
No one except . . .

. . . Earth's most fearsome Commander General.

And there he stands—right between Zot and his Queen . . . and their Attack Ship.

"Stand back!" cries brave Zot.

"Woof!" answers the dreadful General.

"Zot means business!"

"Woof! Woof!" the General insists.

The Queen blinks. It looks like all is lost.

"No!" beeps Zot. "Zot computes a fantastic plan. Plan is . . . ummm . . . well . . . ahh . . . errr . . . Zot will stay and fight. Queen and Best Pal Bot will escape to safeness."

Zot strikes his most intergalactically magnificent pose.

"Remember Zot—Hero Bot."

"Woof, woof!" roars the
horrible General.
Zot booms his last,
most gallant battle cry.

"Hero Zot—never fall.
Hero Zot—conquers all!"
"Yipe!" cries the Commander General, and . . .

. . . he disappears. Once again, Zot is victorious.

"Robot Zot—Brave Bot!
Robot Zot—Hero Bot!"

And so Robot Zot and his Queen zoom off to
distant galaxies to bravely save more days.

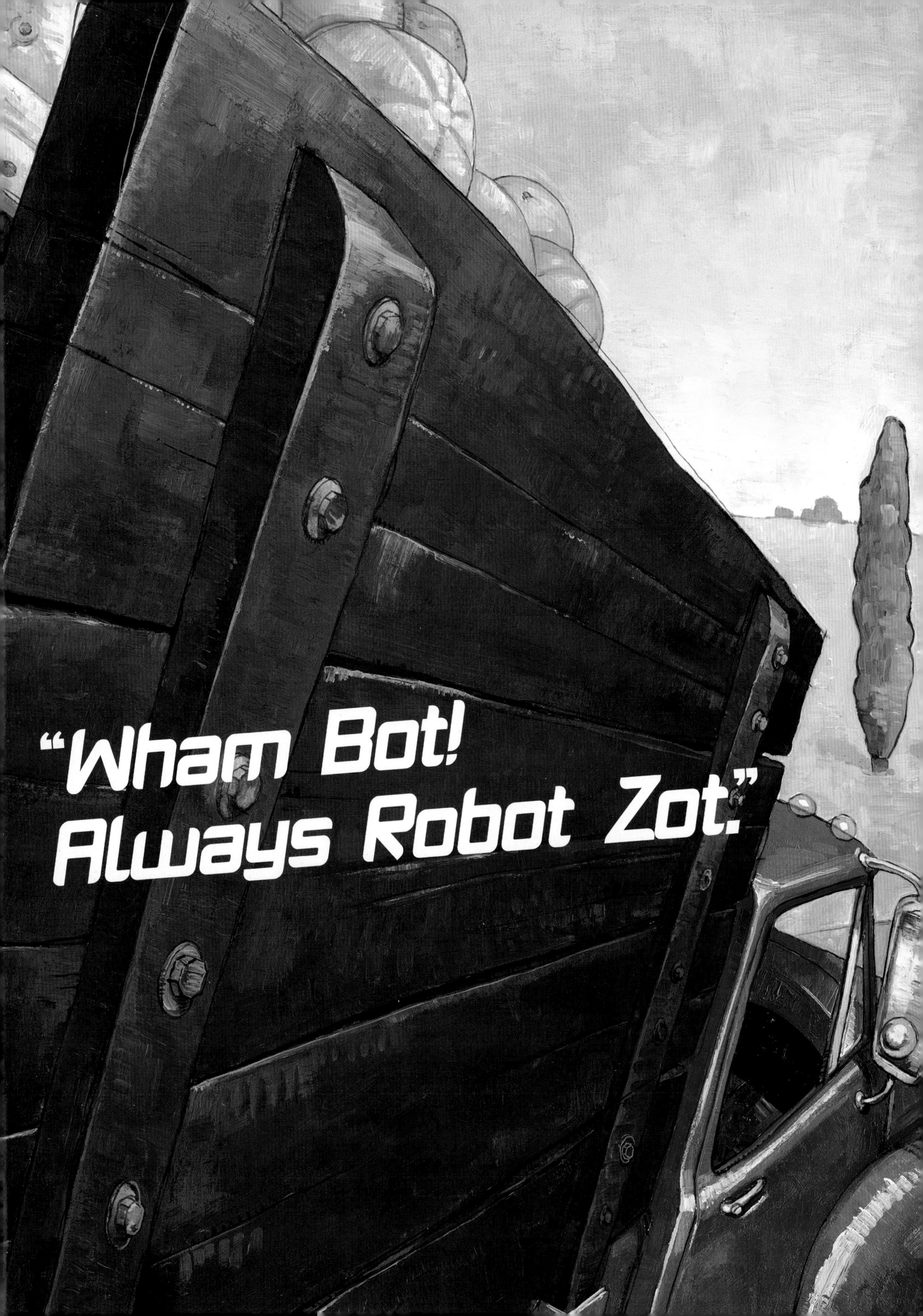
"Wham Bot!
Always Robot Zot."